THE
TOOTH FAIRY
WARS

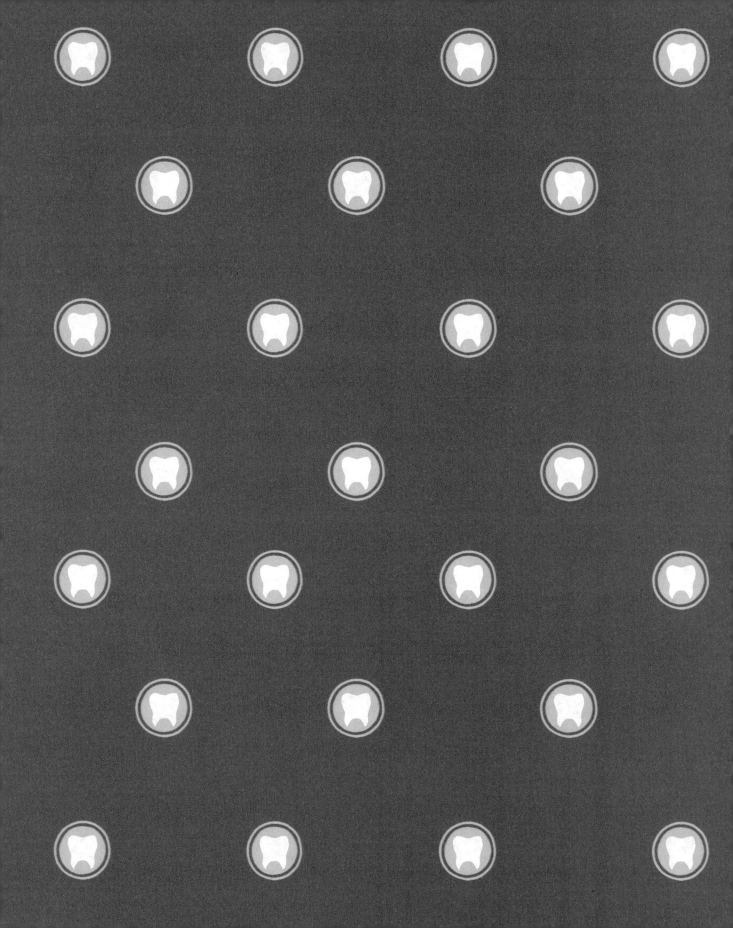

For Dillon, who kept his tooth forever
—K. C.

For Mom
—J. P.

ISBN 978-0-545-83580-0

Text copyright © 2014 by Kathryn Coombs. Illustrations copyright © 2014 by Jake Parker.
All rights reserved. Published by Scholastic Inc., 557 Broadway, New York, NY 10012, by arrangement with Atheneum Books for Young Readers, an imprint of Simon & Schuster Children's Publishing Division.
SCHOLASTIC and associated logos are trademarks and/or registered trademarks of Scholastic Inc.

17 18 19 20/0

40

12 11 10 9 8 7 6 5

Printed in the U.S.A.

First Scholastic printing, January 2015

Book design by Sonia Chaghatzbanian
The text for this book is set in Museo.
The illustrations for this book are rendered in pencil and colored digitally.

THE TOOTH FAIRY WARS

written by **Kate Coombs**
illustrated by **Jake Parker**

SCHOLASTIC INC.

When Nathan lost his first tooth, his mother told him to put it under his pillow. "The Tooth Fairy will come get it, and she'll leave you a dollar!"

"I don't want to," said Nathan. "It's my tooth, and I'm going to keep it forever."

"Hmm," his mom said. "I guess that's okay."

Nathan put the tooth in a plastic bag
and then into his sock drawer.

The Tooth Fairy found it anyway. She was very good
at her job. The Tooth Fairy took Nathan's tooth out of the
baggie, opened her briefcase, and tucked it inside. She left
a dollar behind for Nathan.

In the morning, Nathan was not happy. "It was *my tooth*!" he said.

"I'm sorry, honey," said his mom. "I guess you'll have to hide the next one better."

"The next one?" Nathan asked, worried.

Sure enough, a month later,
another tooth fell out when Nathan
bit into a peanut butter sandwich.

He hid the tooth inside a fort
guarded by army men.

The Tooth Fairy wasn't afraid.
In no time flat, she had traded
Nathan's tooth for a dollar.

When Nathan found the tooth gone,
he growled like a bulldog. He made a better
plan when the third tooth fell out.

That night, after a quick search of Nathan's bedroom, the Tooth Fairy took out her Super Tooth Sensomatic and scanned the house.

She found Nathan's hiding place in the garage, behind some oil cans. "Hmph!" she said to herself as she hurried away to her next stop.

Nathan showed the
dollar to his mother.
  "Again?" She sighed.
"Why don't you try
asking her nicely?"

So when Nathan lost
a fourth tooth, he wrote
the Tooth Fairy a letter.

Dear Tooth Fairy,

I know most kids like to trade you
their teeth for dollars, but
not me. I want to save my
tooth forever.

Your friend,

Nathan

While Nathan slept, the Tooth Fairy came. She read his letter carefully. Then she took the tooth anyway. She left behind a dollar, along with a form letter from her briefcase.

Dear Human Child,

According to Regulation 8439-H, Paragraph 7,
should the dentulous relinquisher object to said
transaction, he or she shall be referred to Office
11 of the Tertiary Fay Division of Rates and
Exchanges, 15th League of Enchanted Commerce.
There, he or she may fill out Form R8, titled
"Petition to Retain Baby Tooth," listing his or
her reasons for requesting an exception to policy,
after which an Adjudication Hearing shall be
held within 25,990 years to decide the case.

Sincerely,

T. Fairy

"25,990 years?" Nathan squawked.

Nathan hid his next tooth inside a carton
full of eggs. The Tooth Fairy found it.
Nathan buried a tooth under the marigolds
in the garden. She got that one too.

He left another tooth at his best friend Danny's house
and put out a cat's tooth he'd found instead.

The Tooth Fairy lost her temper
that night. It took her a long time—
but she tracked down Nathan's tooth.

Nathan tried bribing her. That didn't work.

to: the
Tooth
Fairy

Dear Human Child,

It is strictly against regulations (6120-Q, Paragraph 3) to attempt to bribe an officer of the 15th League of Enchanted Commerce. Please cease and desist at once!

Gravely,

T. Fairy

"Nope," Nathan said.

The next time Nathan lost a tooth, he borrowed his cousin's tarantula. He painted the tooth gray and hid it in the rocks at the bottom of the tarantula tank. Nathan smeared the top of the tank with honey. Then he sprinkled itching powder over the honey and put up some signs.

"Take good care of my tooth, Fred," Nathan told the tarantula as he turned out the light.

Beware DANGER

DANGER KEEP OUT!

When the Tooth Fairy came, she read the signs. She took one look at Fred and turned pale. She sniffed the powdery goo. "Oh my!" she whispered.

The Tooth Fairy did not take Nathan's tooth. She did not leave a dollar. She left a handwritten note instead.

Nathan showed the letter to Danny. "I won!" he yelled.
"What about the substitute?" Danny asked.
"Oh. I'll have to get ready," said Nathan.

The 15th League of Enchanted Commerce
got ready too.
They sent a whole team of Tooth Experts
to Nathan's house.

Poor Tooth Experts!
They tried their best, but it didn't go so well.

The next night, while everybody else in the house was
fast asleep, an official delegation came to see Nathan.

The visitors presented him with a special certificate of exemption and with the contents of Storage Unit 329Z-18 from the Dental Department, 15th League of Enchanted Commerce: every single one of his lost teeth.

"Thanks!" said Nathan. "I'll keep them forever."

And he did.

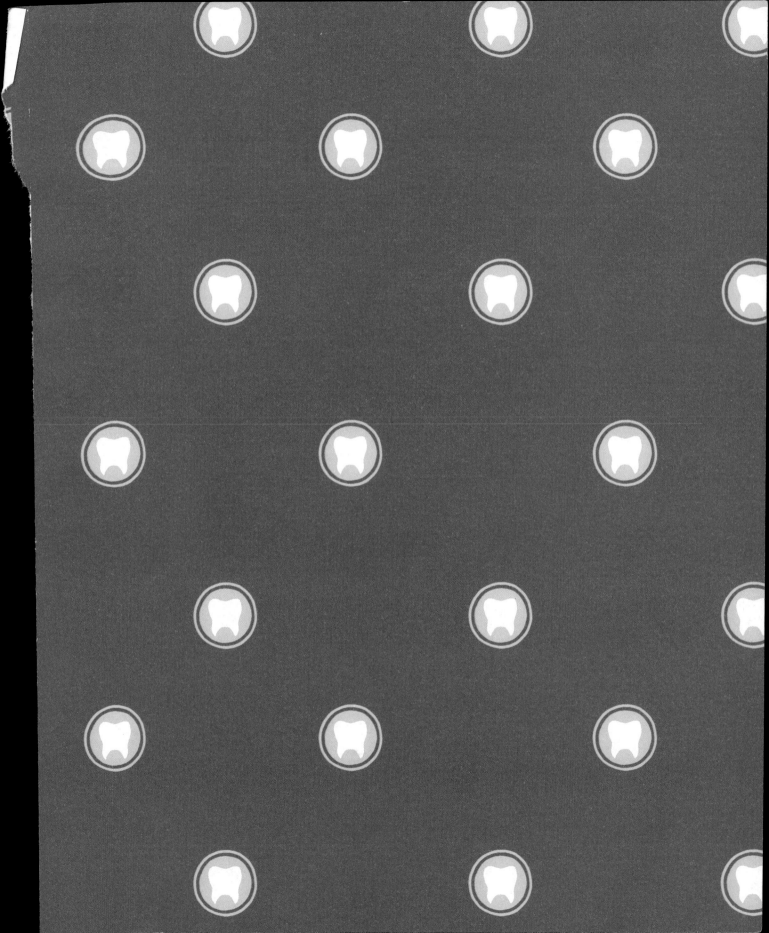